11/11/09 B+J ⁺12.99

Carl's Snowy Afternoon

Alexandra Day

FARRAR STRAUS GIROUX ❄ NEW YORK

*Many thanks to the following helpful people: Emily Anne Allan
and her mother, Nancy; Christina, Rabindranath, and
Sacheverell Darling; Lillian Meyer, Amy Snyder, Scott McKee,
Jeri Wenke, and Patricia Peacock-Evans.*
—A.D.

Copyright © 2009 by Alexandra Day
All rights reserved
Distributed in Canada by Douglas & McIntyre Ltd.
Color separations by Chroma Graphics PTE Ltd.
Printed in February 2009 in China by South China Printing Company Ltd.,
Dongguan City, Guangdong Province
Designed by Irene Metaxatos
First edition, 2009
1 3 5 7 9 10 8 6 4 2

www.fsgkidsbooks.com

Library of Congress Control Number: 2008939063

ISBN-13: 978-0-374-31086-8
ISBN-10: 0-374-31086-6

The Carl character originally appeared in Good Dog, Carl *by
Alexandra Day, published by Green Tiger Press.*

"We're going to the Pond Party with the Parkers. Amy will stay with you. There's a snack in your room."

"I hope that new sitter is reliable."

"Well, Carl's there."

"Why don't you go eat your snack? Then you can play."

"You want to try it, Carl?"

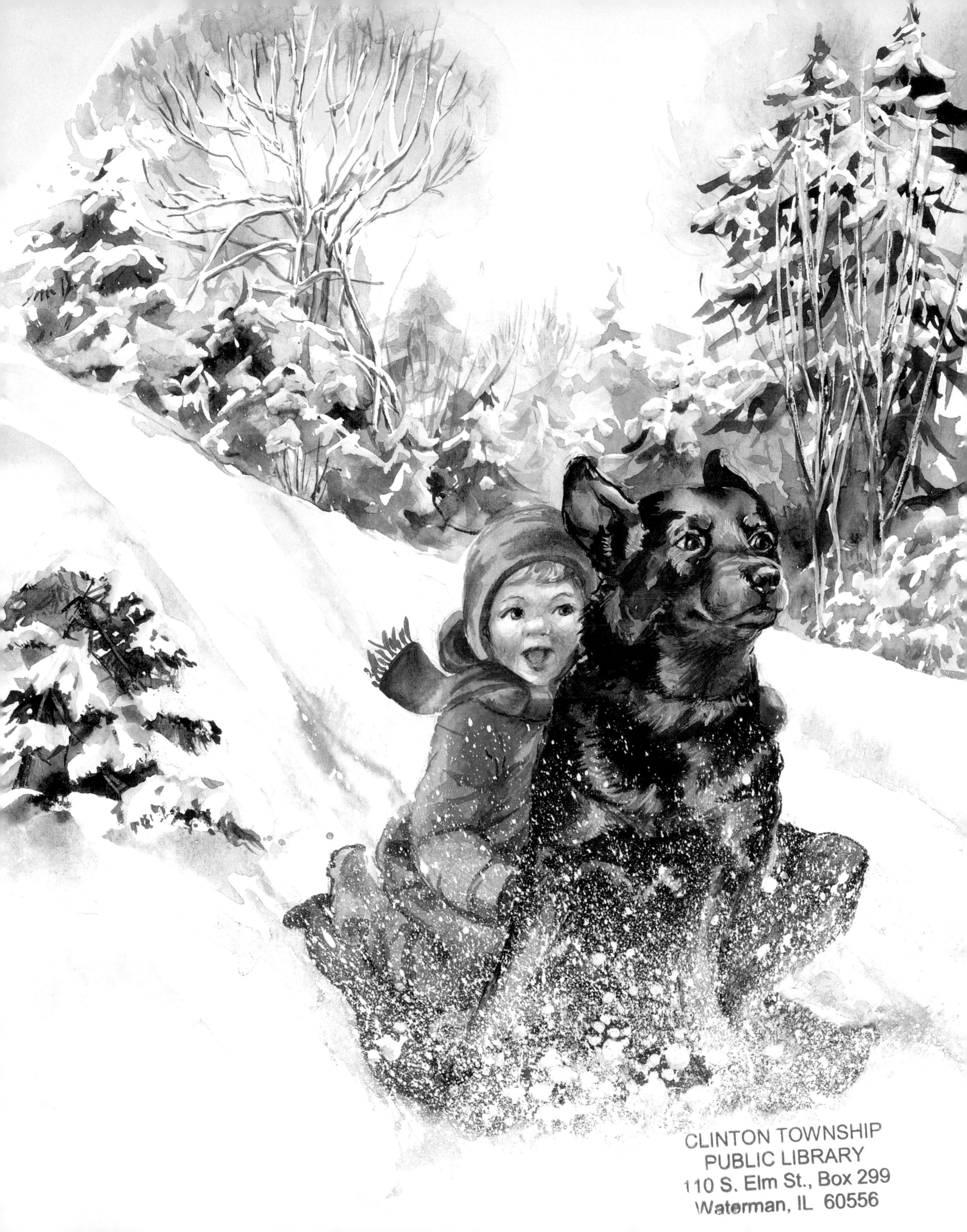

"Come on, Carl, it's fun!"

"Let's stop for some cocoa
on the way home."

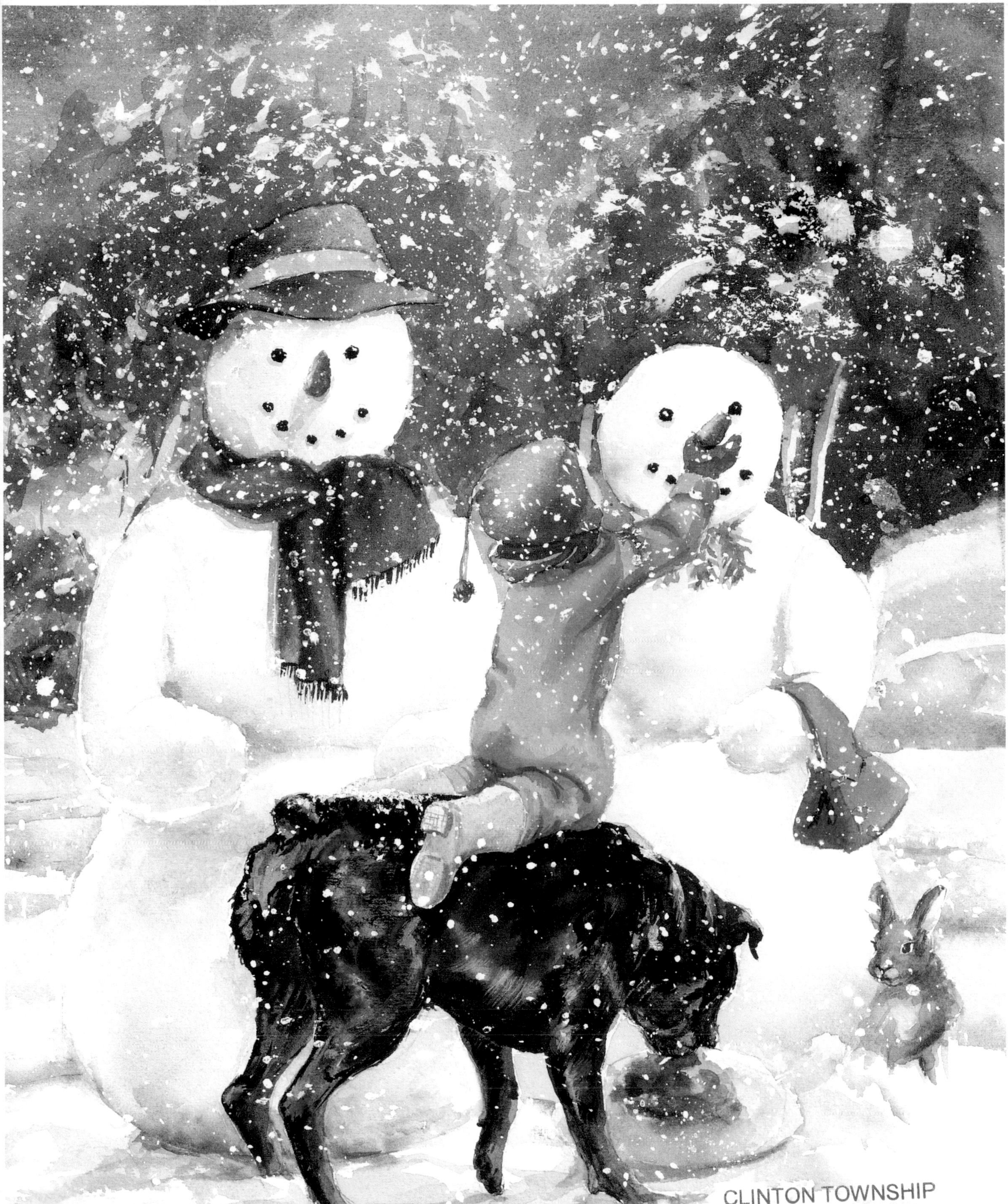

"Did you have a nice time?
Tomorrow you can go out
and play in the snow."